my cousin, the alien

[BOOK #1 OF THE
alien agent]
series

pamela F. service

illustrated by mike gorman

Carolrhoda Books · Minneapolis · New York

Carolrhoda Books
A division of Lerner Publishing Group, Inc.
241 First Avenue North
Minneapolis, MN 55401 U.S.A.

Website address: www.lernerbooks.com

Library of Congress Cataloging-in-Publication Data

Service, Pamela F.
     My cousin, the alien / by Pamela F. Service ; illustrations by Mike Gorman.
          p.   cm. — (Alien agent)
     Summary: While at a resort on a vacation trip his uncle won, Zack begins wondering if his cousin
has been telling the truth for years—that he really is an alien prince sent to Earth for protection, and
who is now being chased by enemy aliens disguised as bald, fat men.
     ISBN 13: 978-0-8225-7627-3 (lib. bdg. : alk. paper)
     [1. Extraterrestrial beings—Fiction. 2. Cousins—Fiction. 3. Identity—Fiction. 4. Science fiction.
5. Humorous stories.] I. Gorman, Mike, ill. II. Title.
PZ7.S4885My 2008
[Fic]—dc22   2007008342

Manufactured in the United States of America
2 3 4 5 6 7 – BP – 14 13 12 11 10 09

For the Indiana Writers Group,
who always had faith in this one

—P.S.

To Danielle,
for your endless love and support

—M.G.

Prologue

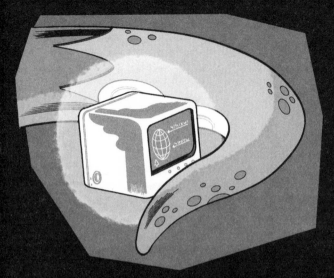

With six of his eyes, Chief Agent Zythis gazed out his window. From his office near the top of the Central Government Tower, the spires and multicolored towers of the Galactic Union capital spread out before him. Transports of all sizes wove through the air.

His other six eyes and most of his attention were trained on his austerely furnished office and the white-haired, purple-skinned humanoid standing there.

"Agent Sorn, thank you for accepting this mission on such short notice. An unexpected crisis has arisen on a planet called Earth. A little out-of-the-way spot, but with a promising species of humanoids. Some years ago, we planted our pre-contact Agent there, but if we don't act quickly, that Agent and the planet's chances of entry into the Galactic Union may be destroyed."

Agent Sorn frowned. "Has this Agent come into his powers yet or been made aware of who he is?"

"No, he's still a child and hopefully has no idea of his real identity. Several years back, we sent a feline agent to check on his progress and had one unfortunate incident of near discovery, but the child was quite young and no ill effects are likely.

Recently, however, we discovered that Gnairt operatives on Earth are tracking him down. Apparently they've been illegally exploiting the planet's resources and are desperate to keep Earth out of the Union so they can continue doing so."

"So our Agent is a threat to them, and they want to abduct or kill him."

Zythis slammed the heaviest of his many tentacles down on his gleaming desk. "Precisely. Your job is to prevent that, hopefully without making the young Agent aware of his status."

With a tentacle tip, he slid an info-cube across to Sorn, its shimmering surfaces concealing a vast store of information. "This will tell you about Earth. You'll need to change skin tones since theirs range from dark brown to pale beige. But white hair is fine; it's a mark of maturity with their species. And please report back at frequent intervals. Any questions?"

Sorn's mind seethed with questions, but she asked only one. "Weaponry?"

"Take plenty. The Gnairt are ruthless and will do anything to keep control over that planet. You're one of our best Agents, Sorn, and the young Agent we planted on Earth has a great deal of potential. Make sure he lives to use it."

CHAPTER ONE

"Zack, I hear your crazy cousin, the alien, is moving back to town in a few weeks," Ken said as he sauntered up to me on the playground, where I was sitting on one of the balance beams.

I gritted my teeth and repeated my mother's line from last night after I'd said almost the same thing to her. "Cousin Ethan's not crazy. He's just ... attention deprived."

Ken raised his eyebrows so they disappeared under his thatch of dark hair. "Well, he sure picks a crazy way to get attention."

"Hey, it's been two years since Ethan lived here. He's probably outgrown that phase." I hated sounding like my mom, but crazy Ethan was family. He was Ethan Gaither and I was Zackary Gaither. I couldn't let anyone outside family get away with calling him crazy.

Ken made little beepy noises, wiggled his fingers on top of his head like antennae, and strolled away.

Grimly I watched. This could destroy what was left of my school year. Of course kids who were new at the school wouldn't remember how Ethan had gone around saying that my Aunt Marsha and Uncle Paul weren't his real parents but were just raising him—an alien abandoned on Earth as a baby. Nothing anyone did could make him admit he was just making it up.

But newcomers also wouldn't remember that when kids used to tease or bully Ethan too much, I'd beat them up. I'm big for my age, and family honor demanded it. Now I might have to prove that to a whole new crop of kids. I never wanted to be the most popular kid in school, but I'd rather not be known as the short-tempered guy with the crazed cousin.

Well, at least this school year only had a

couple more months to go. And anyway, Ethan would be in the grade behind me. Besides, Mom might be right. Maybe he'd outgrown that phase. Maybe he thought he was a Tyrannosaurus rex now.

For the next few weeks, I tried not to think about Ethan. It wasn't easy. Word got around, and people were teasing me already. By the time my uncle, aunt, and cousin did arrive, I would have *preferred* a T. rex.

Uncle Paul's company had bought them a big expensive house and paid for all their stuff to be moved. They spent several days settling in, then came over to our house for dinner. I tried to say I was spending the night at Ken's—or anybody's—but it didn't work.

A car door slammed outside, and moments later, Uncle Paul burst through our door in his typical bull-like style. He laughed and, with one beefy hand, slapped my skinny dad on the back, nearly knocking him over. "Well, here I am, Big Brother, back in your one-horse town. Let me tell you, the company had to promise a hefty raise plus big benefits to lure me back. But I'm worth it, so here I am!"

Before my dad or mom could get a word out, Aunt Marsha fluttered in, wafting her usual cloud of perfume. "Alice, dear, still wearing those colors? Well, I guess one should wear what one likes, whatever the fashion. Still, I do somehow manage both, don't you think? Take this outfit. Isn't it scrumptious?"

She swirled around, looking as always like an escapee from a flashy fashion magazine. I wondered briefly what my aunt really looked like under her extravagant makeup. I think her natural hair color is black, but at the moment it was sort of red gold. The two then bustled my parents into the living room. At least I'd been spared the usual My-how-you've-grown comment. But then, Aunt Marsha and Uncle Paul never noticed kids much.

Including their own. I looked down the front path, and there was Ethan walking up very slowly. He'd grown a little taller, I guess, but he was still pale and skinny.

"Hi," he said, a shy smile flicking across the solemn face I remembered all too well. "If you don't want to sit around listening to my parents brag, let's go to your room."

Once up there, he shoved some comic books off my desk chair, plopped down, and started spinning. That much hadn't changed. Once he'd told me that seeing my posters for bands and movies spin by in colored swirls made him feel like he was traveling (again) through hyperspace. Right.

"So, how are things?" I asked when the spinning slowed. Pretty lame, but it was all I could think of.

"Okay, but I'm glad we're back here. Big cities are scary."

Right, I thought. *Particularly if you try to tell tough big-city kids that you're an alien*. Out loud I asked, "How was the school there?"

"Horrendous. After a while, my folks put me in a private school. Not much better, and I had to board there when both of them were out of town. Dad was sent to bunches of foreign places, and Mom went along. Not me, though."

"Bummer."

He nodded, his white-blond hair slipping over his eyes. "Yeah, but I've traveled across the galaxy. I suppose I don't have to see Paris."

My heart sank. "You're still . . . telling people you're an alien?"

He gave me a look like I was the stupidest thing on Earth. "No way. I was a little kid then. Didn't have good sense." His eyes flashed with intensity, and he hunched forward. "You know what my parents did? They sent me to a therapist."

About time, I thought, but kept quiet.

"The guy said I had 'changeling syndrome.'" Ethan imitated a snooty adult voice. "'A common malady of maladjusted children or ones from dysfunctional families where the child claims to be adopted and to not really belong to the natural parents. A classic cry for attention.'"

With a kick against my desk, Ethan sent

the chair into an angry spin. "It's that shrink who's maladjusted! Anyone can see I don't belong to my so-called parents. They're tall and dark, and I'm small and light. And our personalities are totally different! They come on strong enough to knock over an elephant, and I like to just sit back and think. We're not even interested in the same things."

"Sure, but that doesn't mean . . . "

"Not by itself, maybe, but I *am* an alien. I've always known that. Or at least I have since that time with the cat."

"The cat?"

"The fluffy yellow cat we saved from the Doberman."

"Oh, right." I vaguely remembered that when we were both pretty little, playing in my backyard, we'd saved a stray cat from a mean neighborhood dog. Afterward we'd both pretended the cat had talked to us. We'd played it was a secret space alien.

"But that was just a game," I protested.

"Wasn't! I'd already figured out that since I

was so different from my parents, I was probably adopted. The cat just confirmed that. Do you remember what it said?"

"We *pretended* it said 'Thanks' and some other stuff."

"It said, 'Thanks. I'm sent to check on you, and you end up saving me.' We both heard it."

"We both pretended we did. I was busy slamming the gate on that dog."

"And I was holding the cat." Ethan smiled triumphantly. "That's when I felt it had wings tucked under its fur."

"What?"

"I didn't say anything then, but I thought about it lots and realized it must have been an alien. Then suddenly that explained everything. I'd never felt like I belonged because I was an alien too! And anyway, the pendant confirms it. I was wearing it that day, so maybe that's how the cat knew me."

I groaned as he tugged at the chain around his neck. His stupid pendant was a shimmery holographic disk dotted with silvery bumps and one multi-colored crystal. Actually, it *was* cool looking, but not necessarily alien.

"I've had this as long as I can remember. It must have been given to me by my alien parents when they left me with these people."

"But," I pointed out, "your mother said it's just a trinket that caught your eye somewhere when you were a baby."

"Of course, they'd say that. They don't want anyone to know the truth. That used to make me mad, but now I've figured out that they're right."

"You mean you don't . . . "

He gave me that look again. "They need to hide the fact that I'm an alien. That's why I'm here, see? I'm being hidden. Maybe from other aliens. Bad aliens. Maybe I'm a prince of one interstellar empire being hidden from a rival empire. That's why it was stupid of me to go around telling people I'm an alien. So now I'm keeping it a secret within my adopted family."

"Oh," I said. "That's smart, I guess."

And there it was, I realized. He was working his spell on me again. Ethan sounded and looked so sincere when he said that stuff, he could almost make me believe it too. He'd always been good at imagination games. We'd play time-traveling dinosaur hunters or swashbuckling pirates, and I'd get totally swept up in it. Even when his teachers gave him poor grades, they always marked that he had "a fertile imagination."

When I was littler, I'd thought it was cool having a maybe-alien cousin. That's before he started school too, and I had to put up with the other kids' reactions. Well, he could believe whatever he wanted, as long as he kept quiet about it. Maybe I wouldn't have to bloody so many noses defending him this year.

That Monday, I felt almost relaxed about Ethan starting school, even when he strode through the noisy cafeteria heading for the table where I was eating lunch with Ken and Sean. Sean was new to our school, but Ken was already snickering. I shot him a squelching look.

Ethan plunked his tray beside mine and slid onto the bench. I wanted to tell him to eat with his own grade, but I knew he hadn't had a chance yet to make new friends, and he certainly wouldn't have any among those kids who'd known him before. So I introduced him, keeping a stern eye on Ken. We ate, talked, and traded various bits of unwanted food. I swapped my soggy taco for Sean's cheese sandwich. I like cheese.

But just before the bell, William Smothers swaggered up, a big smirk on his freckled face. This kid might look like your typical jolly redhead, but he's one of the nastiest bullies in creation.

"Well, if it isn't that little twerp from outer space. Been off visiting the mother ship, have you? Still pushing that crazy stuff about being an alien?"

I scowled, readying my fist under the table. Ethan threw William a quick, cold smile. "You're the crazy one. If I *was* an alien and you were that rude to me, I'd zap you with my disintegrator ray. But I haven't, see? So how could I be an alien?"

Ethan raised both hands—innocently empty. William glowered at him and then at me. I raised my hands too, one in a fist.

At that point, I decided, quite wrongly, that this year wouldn't be so bad after all.

CHAPTER TWO

For the next several weeks, a few more kids hassled Ethan about the alien thing, but he just turned it around, like *they* were the crazy ones. He even began making friends in his own grade and ate lunch with them. I finally decided that family honor was safe, and I could get on with my life. I wasn't even too put out when at dinner one night Mom announced, while passing the vegetables, that Aunt Marsha had called, and Ethan would be spending Saturday with us.

My mom's usually calm about stuff, and so is my dad—most of the time. In fact, people say

I'm a rather calm kid too. So that's one way we three are alike, as well as all of us having brown hair, muddy brown eyes, and a deep love for cheese in all its forms.

But Mom's announcement set my dad off. "Watch out, Alice, they'll be starting that again!"

"Starting what, dear?" my mom said, spooning out broccoli and passing me her special cheese sauce.

Dad drummed his fingers on the table. "Sending Ethan over to our place all the time. You'd think people with that much money could afford a babysitter! But Paul and Marsha figure they can impose on us because we're family."

"They aren't imposing," Mom answered. "And anyway, we *are* family."

"Well, if they spent a little more time with their own kid, maybe he wouldn't be so . . ." His voice trailed off as he glanced at me. His grumble dropped a notch. "Anyway, of course Ethan can come over—if it's all right with Zack. He's the one who'll have to put up with the kid."

I smiled weakly around my broccoli. "Sure, we can find stuff to do." Chewing, I wondered if we could do normal stuff or if he'd be on that alien kick again. Well, I'd treat it as a game, and maybe someday he would too.

When Ethan arrived Saturday morning, I was in the garden halfheartedly weeding radishes. I figured weeds had as much right to live as radishes did, but Mom didn't see it that way.

Ethan stalked into our backyard with a high-magnitude scowl and began griping. "You'd think those human parents of mine would be honored that they're raising an alien prince. You'd think they'd respect the ways I'm different. But you know what they've done? They've hired a tutor so that I can waste every afternoon studying stuff I can't learn."

Ethan's grades had always been mixed, with lots of bad in that mix. In fact, if he hadn't been teased for being the school wacko, he might have been teased for being the school dunce. So for the sake of family honor, a tutor might be a good idea, though saying that to him wouldn't exactly be diplomatic.

"Well, if you give it a try, they'll probably stop bugging you about schoolwork," I said, adding a handful of withered weeds to my little stack.

Ethan snorted. "My species is good at some subjects and not others. Why fight it?" he said with a shrug. Ethan had squatted down and was pretending to study the little seed packet propped on a stick at the end of the garden row. But I could tell the subject of tutors wasn't being shrugged off.

"But maybe if you tried . . ."

"Why? Dogs are good at barking but can't fly no matter how hard they try. I'm good at math and science, but social studies and spelling just don't work for me. Different species do different things. It's inherent. Let's go to the mall."

Subject closed. This pretending he was an alien might be maddening for everybody else, but it sure was handy for him. Don't like a subject in school? Your species doesn't do it. Period.

Anyway, I wasn't grumbling as we headed to the mall. Ethan always had plenty of money, and I never did. His parents might not spend a lot of time with him, but they didn't neglect his finances.

We headed straight for the pizza place. Guzzling down extra-cheese pizza and sodas, we watched puppies climbing over each other in the pet store window. Then we went to the bookstore. Ethan got himself a couple of game books and bought me the latest in the *Spacerats* series.

Next came a computer store. "I'm looking for a new screen saver," he explained. "Dad got me the stupid fish, but I'd like the one where you're flying through space at warp speed. It'd make me feel at home." He stopped to examine a display.

"You're on the Internet, I guess?" I asked with a pang of jealousy.

"Of course. Aren't you?" He looked at me

like I was the alien.

"Not yet. Not at home, anyway. My dad says you can waste a whole life that way."

He snorted. "Or you can *get* a whole life. It's great what you can learn on it."

"Ever look up websites about UFOs?" Maybe that's where he got his ideas.

Ethan grunted. "I wouldn't log onto anything like that."

"Why not?"

Again, I got that how-dumb-can-you-be look. "Because aliens would have ways to trace what people log onto. I'm in hiding, remember? If the bad aliens are looking for me on Earth, they'll check which people are interested in aliens and UFOs. I can't risk it."

I laughed. "Wouldn't they have better things to do?"

He looked around, checking to make sure nobody could overhear. "We don't know what information they already have. Suppose they know the Imperial Prince is hidden in this country, or even this town? I've got to be careful."

I felt myself slipping into his game again. "Careful of what?"

"Of attracting too much attention—particularly from strangers. Like those two guys over there. No, don't turn around! I noticed them outside the pet store, and now they're outside this place. Forget the screen saver—that'd be a dead giveaway anyhow. Let's go."

Abruptly he left the store and began striding down the mall. I followed, wanting to look behind, but I didn't. I remembered the time years ago when Ken and I played we were secret agents and followed people around the mall, pretending they were foreign spies. We thought we were pretty secretive until a couple of jerks threatened to call mall security on us.

Ethan was good at this. He weaved through the crowd then dodged into a department store. Turning right at the perfume department, he pushed through racks of flowery blouses as if they were jungle plants and we were being chased by raptors.

Then we broke into a clearing. Housewares.

"Too exposed here," Ethan whispered. He ducked into the towel section, keeping to the valleys between shelves until we reached lingerie, and bolted for the store's other doorway. A couple of ladies pursed their lips as we rushed by, but nobody called security.

"Did we ditch them?" I asked as we moved back into the flow of people. I'd totally surrendered to the game.

"For the moment," Ethan whispered. "But let's hide in here for a while."

A toy store. Good plan. At the action figures, Ethan concentrated on superheroes, avoiding aliens and spacemen. He sure took this thing to extremes.

After moving to computer games and checking those out, Ethan said, "Come on, we'd better keep moving."

Out among the river of shoppers again, I was about to suggest we could keep moving just as easily with ice cream cones in our hands when Ethan whispered, "There they are again, on that bench. Act casual."

As we walked by, I casually glanced at the benches. On one, a mother was changing a baby's diaper. On the other, a couple of guys were sitting, both bald and bulbously fat. They looked like better candidates for foreign spies than aliens, but this was Ethan's game.

We strolled to the food court, ideal for losing ourselves in the crowd. Also ideal for ice cream. Armed at last with cones, we found a bench concealed by a drooping potted tree and concentrated on our chocolate swirl and blueberry crunch. We'd slurped down to cone level when Ethan whispered, "There they are again. They're persistent."

I looked where he gestured with his dripping cone. A couple of fat, bald guys were buying egg rolls. They looked a lot like each other, but I wasn't sure if they were the same ones we'd seen before. That made them a good choice for the game, I guess. The world is full of fat, bald guys.

Ethan stuffed the last of his cone into his mouth and headed down another branch of the mall. As I caught up, he said thickly, "This calls for evasive maneuvers."

Darting sideways, he pushed through a doorway marked "Employees Only."

I nearly panicked as the door shut behind him. He'd be caught. Someone would call security for sure. Still, he was my younger cousin, crazy or not, and if anyone ever needed protecting, even from himself, it was Ethan. Glancing around, I slipped through the door too.

It was a narrow hallway, drab and dim compared to the bright bustling mall outside. No smell of nachos and scented candles in here— just damp cardboard and cleaning fluids. On my left was a small closet with sink, buckets, and mops. "Ethan," I whispered urgently as I walked on. No answer.

The hallway turned a corner. A single ceiling bulb lit the empty stretch in front of me. "Ethan?" A faint noise came from somewhere ahead.

Scarcely daring to breath, I tiptoed on. A

door on my right was partially open. Pushing it, I saw a forest of bristly Christmas trees. Nestled among them was Santa's gold throne with cousin Ethan perched upon it.

"Cool hideout, huh?" he said cheerily. "We could stay here until the aliens stop looking for me. Or better yet, we could stay until the mall closes and then walk around it at night."

"That's a bad idea, Ethan," I said stamping out a sudden spark of temptation.

"Sure is," said a gruff man's voice. "A really bad idea."

I spun around and stared. A fat, bald guy stood in the doorway.

CHAPTER THREE

Agent Sorn looked at herself critically in the dressing room mirror. Her lovely purple skin was now boring native beige, but at least it wouldn't clash with the hideous clothes she'd picked up as an excuse to use the store's dressing room. Not that she planned to try them on. She just needed someplace private to transmit her report.

After disabling the security camera, she brought out her sender and began.

"I've located our Agent. He and another youngster, a relative, spent part of the day in a large commercial complex. I also believe I have identified two Gnairt agents. They seem to have a device by which they can home in on our Agent, but apparently it is not precise. It led them only to his general vicinity. I don't believe they have identified him yet. I will attempt to misdirect them with a diffuser."

Sorn examined several other devices in her satchel, lingering briefly on a trim silvery laser gun.

She continued. "Hopefully violence can be averted. Oddly, our Agent may have some sense of danger. He and his relative carried out impressive evasive maneuvers when near the Gnairt. Possibly, the earlier encounter you reported with our feline agent had some lingering effect. I will attempt to manipulate situations to move our Agent beyond the Gnairt's detection range in hopes that they will abandon their pursuit. Agent Sorn out."

Slipping the sender into her satchel, Sorn again examined one boldly-patterned garment then fought down a laugh as she imagined Chief Agent Zythis wearing the thing. It would need a lot more arm holes.

She held the native garment up to herself,

studying the mirror. Still, it wouldn't hurt to try it on. Might even help with her disguise. Gnairt were a tricky enemy and always suspicious. She had to be careful not to tip them off. This assignment could be more dangerous than she'd first thought.

Minutes later, looking at herself in the human dress, she shrugged. Not bad really. This assignment could also have its compensations— if she didn't get herself or her charge killed.

CHAPTER FOUR

Ethan leaped from the throne and looked around like a trapped animal.

The fat, bald man leaned his broom against a wall and said, "What are you kids doing in here anyway? Didn't you read the 'Employees Only' sign?"

He was looking at me like I was the responsible adult. "Er, yes . . . sort of. But we were . . . looking for restrooms and figured there'd be some in here."

"Sure there are, but they're for 'Employees Only.' Get it? Come on, I'll point you to the public ones."

He stood aside so we could squeeze out past his belly. Then he herded us down a different hallway to a closed door. The fat, bald, and probably very human guy in the janitor's uniform opened the door to the bright, bustling mall.

"Public restrooms by the exit. And kids, don't try staying here overnight. We've got security men patrolling the place. You'd get in big trouble."

"Don't worry, we won't," I said. "It was just a game, anyway."

And it had been a fun game, I admitted to myself as we headed home. The one thing that kept nagging me was that I wasn't sure my crazy cousin thought it was a game.

Weeks went by, and I was definitely not upset that I didn't see much of Ethan now that he was being tutored after school. You can only take so much of crazy people, family or not. Then came the invitation to "the Big Show-Off Party." My dad called it that, ranting that it was just Uncle Paul's "showing off his posh new house to all the other snobs in town—and showing how much better he's done in life than his brother."

"Stop talking like that," my mom objected. "You know very well that Paul loves you and you love him."

"Of course I love him! He's family. I just think he's a jerk!"

We went, of course, despite Dad's blusterings. When Mom tried to help in the kitchen, she got chased out by cooks and maids. Then she and Dad were whisked off by Aunt Marsha for a grand tour, leaving me in the hall facing Ethan under a huge light hung with crystal blobs.

"Four hundred and thirty-nine," he said, catching my stare. "I counted. Yeah, I know, this house is majorly ostentatious. But it's got some okay stuff too. I'll show you."

Ethan always liked using big words. An "ostentatious" habit, but I didn't point that out.

And his room *was* pretty cool with its floor-to-ceiling windows and massive computer equipment. I noticed that among all the posters covering the wall there wasn't a single scene from a space movie. A pretend alien in hiding sure loses out on a lot.

After showing me the wonders of his room, the rest of the mansion, the four-car garage, and the formal gardens, Ethan led me to the food tables beside the swimming pool. Despite disapproving glares from the guys in white coats serving the food, Ethan demonstrated how to build a cracker wall around the edge of the little plastic plates so they could hold more food. With scientifically piled plates, we settled into a couple of deck chairs half-hidden by a giant outdoor umbrella. Around us, the talking, laughing, posing adults were paying attention only to themselves.

After a while of silent stuffing, I asked, "So how's this tutoring thing? Really bad?"

"No," he said, sticking black olives on all his fingers. "I can ignore the tutor just like I ignore teachers. But it's infuriating—a waste of time." One by one, he sucked the olives into his mouth. "My parents and I keep fighting about it. Last night, Mom yelled that if

I loved her, I'd try to learn something, and I yelled that if they loved me, they'd stop trying to make me learn that stuff. Our two species don't communicate very well."

I tried not to sound too nerdy. "Maybe they think that wanting you to do well in school shows they do love you? I mean, adults are always lecturing about getting good grades so we can get good jobs. Your dad probably wants you to make lots of money like he does instead of like my dad."

"But I don't care about all that. See? That's another way I'm not like them. My *real* parents would love me without always bringing money into it."

He suddenly lowered his voice so I could barely hear it above the chattering crowd. "Even throwing a party like this is dangerous. If they loved me and cared about keeping me safe, they wouldn't do it."

"What do you mean?" The party looked harmless to me. Just a bunch of adults standing around talking and trying to impress each other.

"They're calling attention to us. They invited all the town's bigwigs, but they don't know half of these people. An alien looking for the hidden Imperial Prince could slip in easily. It could be any of those people—like that fat, bald guy by the bar."

I checked the guy out and almost choked laughing. "Not that one, Ethan. That's the Mayor."

"Could be a cover identity," he huffed.

Standing up, he threw his empty plastic plate like a Frisbee into the garbage can. "Never mind, let's go swimming."

The rest of the evening was okay. Ethan didn't accuse any other prominent citizens of being aliens. And his indoor/outdoor pool was amazing.

Next morning my dad made a surprise announcement over our cheese omelet breakfast. Our kitchen wasn't as grand as Ethan's, but our crowded little breakfast nook was cozy. "Believe it or not, *want* it or not," he intoned, "we're taking a vacation."

"What?" my mother asked, nearly dropping her fork.

"Where?" I asked.

"And why?" my dad grumbled. "Because my little brother wants to show off again."

After a long pause, my mother prodded him. "Meaning . . . ?"

"Meaning Paul told me last night that he won some surprise drawing, and his company is giving him an all-expense-paid stay at Deer Springs Resort for his family and another family of his choice. He chose us."

I let out a whoop. Mom and I exchanged big grins. I didn't have a clue about Deer Springs Resort, but it sounded better than our usual vacations in run-down motels.

Mom cocked an eyebrow. "I hope you had the good sense *not* to turn him down."

Dad glowered. "Yeah, I swallowed my pride and accepted. But I only did it for you two! Otherwise I wouldn't go near that rich snobs' playground—particularly not on my brother's charity."

"It isn't charity, dear, it's family togetherness. When do we go?"

Turns out we were going the week after school let out and staying in the place for five days with our rooms, meals, and use of all the resort facilities paid for. Maybe five solid days with my crazy cousin would be a little too much togetherness. But once Dad showed me the resort brochure, I figured I could stand it. Horseback riding, swimming pools, incredible gardens, and a building right out of fantasy stories. Fantastic and very Earthly looking.

Maybe we would spend the whole time without thinking about aliens.

Amazing how wrong I could be.

CHAPTER FIVE

It took several hours to drive to Deer Springs Resort. The brochure said that it was once one of the poshest hotels in the country, and lots of rich, famous people bathed in its mineral springs to get healthy, then drank bottled "Vulcan Wasser" to cure just about everything.

Maybe I'd been thinking too much about aliens lately, but Vulcan Wasser reminded me of TV space people. The brochure said Vulcan was the old Roman god of volcanoes, and *wasser* was German for water. Whatever.

The hotel was really big, or as Ethan called it, "gargantuan." It had columns everywhere like a huge wedding cake. Guys in red uniforms hauled our luggage up the wide front stairs. The enormous lobby sprouted potted palms, thick marble columns, and crystal chandeliers.

Once we'd checked in, a young guy in a uniform piled our luggage onto a cart and led us into a creaky elevator that, after a slow, noisy, and very cramped trip, opened again on the top floor. Our rooms were at one end of a long hall. Each family had a huge master bedroom with a bathroom grand enough for an emperor. Ethan and I each had our own bedrooms next to our parents' with our own doors to the hall. The windows showed rambling gardens and another wing of the hotel that was covered with scaffolding.

We unpacked and went downstairs to a restaurant so fancy I was sure I'd do something wrong. There were white tablecloths, candles, cloth napkins folded like peacocks' tails, and pieces of silverware I hadn't a clue how to use. The menu prices were scary too, but since it was already paid for, I ordered lobster.

It looked gross but tasted okay. Ethan had steak. Maybe he thought lobsters looked too much like aliens.

He certainly did not like the fat, bald waiter and whispered dire warnings to me. He watched the guy like a hawk when he served our food in case he pulled out some paralyzing weapon or sprinkled radioactive poison on our salads. But in a hotel that, like my dad said, caters to rich, middle-aged golfers, Ethan would either have to get used to seeing fat, bald guys or pick another game. After dinner even Ethan relaxed, and the six of us were so stuffed we just sat in rocking chairs on the big hotel porch and made plans for tomorrow.

Turned out, it rained buckets the next day, so Ethan and I stopped arguing about whether to go horseback riding or swimming and explored the hotel instead. Our moms took mud baths at the hotel spa, and our dads went bowling.

This hotel demanded a lot of exploring. Ethan might be scared of enemy aliens, but he sure wasn't scared of doing things we probably weren't supposed to. We took back stairs, slipped through unmarked doors, and explored areas roped off for renovation.

In one corridor, we saw a heavy guy who was kind of balding step out of his room. Like a scared cat, Ethan ducked into an alcove, opened a window, and stepped onto the fire escape.

"Hey, you can't do that," I whispered sharply.

"Why not? These things are made for people to escape from danger."

"Yeah, but they look plenty dangerous themselves." And they did. All rusty and covered with pigeon droppings.

"You scared?" He was already climbing down. I was scared, but even more scared that Ethan would hurt himself, and it'd be my fault for not watching out for him. So I followed. You could see through the slatted metal steps all the way to the ground. They swayed and creaked with every step. It wasn't raining just then, but the rusty steps and hand rails were wet and slippery.

Ethan wanted to keep going, but I stopped at the next floor. "Look, that guy probably caught an elevator to the bottom. Let's duck in here. He'd never think of looking for us just one floor down."

"He won't think of looking on the fire escape either."

I stayed put. "How come you're scared of getting on a horse but you don't mind scrambling around dozens of feet off the ground?"

"Maybe my planet has lots of mountains, but we don't ride on big snorting animals."

Okay, I could think fast too. "So, what if that alien guesses we took the fire escape and starts climbing up from the bottom?"

"Then I'd pull out my pendant and see if I can make it work as a weapon." He yanked at the chain until the weird metal disk was swinging against his chest. "I keep thinking that if I press the bumps in the right order, the crystal will fire a death ray or something. But I haven't found the order yet."

I looked at the shimmering pendant. The

bumps seemed scattered with no pattern at all. "Have you tried drawing lines between them to see if they make a picture, like connect-the-dots?"

"Yeah. It just makes a mess."

A raindrop bounced off the disk, and several more off my head. "Let's go in. If we're soaked at lunch, our folks will know we didn't stay inside like they told us."

The rain was getting more serious as we struggled to open the window. Finally we forced it up in a shower of dust and dry paint flakes. Dramatically, Ethan scanned the empty corridor, then gestured for us to slide in. If I could just get over feeling overprotective, I admitted to myself, this game could almost be fun.

After lunch, which fortunately had no bald waiters, the adults went to play tennis in the indoor pavilion. Ethan and I just sprawled on the plush couches in the lobby, feeling a little heavy after our triple-decker sandwiches, fries, and large chocolate sundaes.

Even so, sitting out in the open like this,

Ethan made us take turns being on guard. One of us would sit up watching for enemies while the other lay back in an overfed stupor and stared at the fancy ceiling. It was painted with cupids and with people wearing flowing bed sheets and riding chariots. They were surrounded by stars connected by gold lines forming constellations.

"You know," I said lazily from where I was slumped amid big squishy pillows. "That pattern of stars over there looks sort of like the dots on your pendant."

Ethan swiveled his gaze from suspicious doorways to the ceiling. "It does! Maybe that's the secret of the pendant? It's not only a weapon, it's a map showing where I'm from! What constellation is that?"

"Don't know. Maybe there's a star guide in the gift shop."

In seconds, Ethan was off to the hotel gift shop, where he snapped up a nature guide on stars. Back on the couch, we began thumbing through the book comparing the constellation patterns with the dots on the pendant. None quite fit.

I had to look at everything sideways, because he was hogging the book. "You know," I said as he turned another page, "if you look at that one sideways and count all those little dots too, that might be it."

Ethan stared from the pendant to the page and back again. "That's it! If the crystal is where the book shows the star Rigel, then the pendant's pattern is Orion. Maybe I come from some planet of Rigel's? I'm a Rigelian!"

Ethan practically glowed with happiness. His belief in this alien thing was contagious. "Okay," I said. "Tonight we'll go out and look for Rigel. It's stopped raining."

Sunlight, having finally torn free from the clouds, was slicing through the lobby's tall windows. Others had noticed the weather change too. A couple guys were already marching through the lobby toward the front door, golf bags over their shoulders. I wished they weren't fat and bald—and that they hadn't stared at us like we were littering the lobby.

As they looked our way, Ethan hurriedly palmed his pendant and stuffed the star book into a pocket. "Right. More evasion. Let's duck out the back way. Plenty of exploring to do outside."

The newly appeared sun was turning the rain-soaked gardens into a giant steam bath. Funny how you don't notice air-conditioning until you're away from it.

The gardens were certainly fancy. One had masses of rosebushes and smelled like, well, masses of roses. Another had hedges cut into animal shapes, and beyond that sprawled a Japanese garden. Near the Japanese place we noticed a peculiar, nasty smell, kind of like rotten eggs. It wafted from a small round building, if you can call something with only pillars for walls a building. I remembered the picture in the brochure.

"There's the Vulcan Wasser Pavilion."

As we walked closer, the smell got worse.

Inside the circle of pillars, a brick patio surrounded a tiled basin. We looked into it.
Bubbles rose through brownish water, each one
bursting with a new little stink.

"You mean, people actually took baths in
that?" Ethan said. "Of their own free will?"

I nodded. "And drank it to cure stuff.
Probably it just made people sick so they had
to buy medicine the hotel sold."

The only other person in the pavilion just
then was a white-haired lady sitting on a
bench reading. She looked up and laughed.
"Vulcan Wasser was supposed to be good for
everything from cancer to arthritis. People
can talk themselves into believing some pretty
crazy things."

"They sure can," I said firmly as I watched
Ethan drop pebbles into the pool. I wished I
could find some cure for him—something so
he'd know he was an okay kid without having
to pretend he was an alien.

I had a sudden urge to talk with the white-
haired lady about it. She gave off this glow

of being kind and wise. But that was stupid. She was a total stranger. And anyway, a family came into the pavilion just then. Two giggling little kids ran in holding their noses and making noisy jokes about the stink. The lady smiled at us like we three were mature adults sharing a joke. Ethan and I left, feeling far superior to those crude rugrats.

We headed back to the Japanese garden with its ferns and miniature temples. Crossing an arched bridge, we watched humongous goldfish cruising through the shallow green water.

"There must be a fortune down there!" Ethan said excitedly.

"Goldfish are expensive?" I said, confused.

"No, dummy, the coins."

He was right. The scattered pebbles sparkling in the sun were really coins. Pennies mostly, but silver ones too.

Ethan turned to me, eyes glittering like the coins. "Suppose we sneak out here at night and kind of clean up their pond for them? I mean, the people already got their good luck when they threw the money in."

The coins glinted temptingly like lost Spanish doubloons. "Could work," I admitted. "Both our rooms have separate doors to the hall."

"Done! A major nighttime adventure, then wealth beyond our wildest dreams!"

Probably not. I have some pretty wild dreams. But at least this adventure was firmly planted on Earth. Lost pirate treasure. Nothing to do with aliens or ever-present fat, bald guys.

You'd think warning bells would go off when I think comfortable thoughts like that.

CHAPTER SIX

That night it was too cloudy to go looking for Ethan's supposed home star. But the treasure hunt was still on. I'd been pretty sleepy after dinner, but the idea of a forbidden night-time adventure woke me up. And, of course, it would have been forbidden, had we asked—which is why we didn't.

It took forever to get the adults upstairs and into bed. I crawled almost fully dressed into the canopy bed in my own room, then lay there listening to my parents' water running and toilet flushing. When things finally quieted down next door, I gave them fifteen more minutes, then donned shoes and jacket and slipped into the hall.

Ethan was already there, sitting on a cold radiator. "My folks always check on me once before they go to bed. But now we're clear."

We headed down the stairwell at the end of the hall, plain cement stairs, not like the wide carpeted ones in the center of the building. We didn't meet anybody.

Once we passed through the door at the bottom, the air-conditioned quiet of the hotel gave way to warm, damp air full of sound. Things chirped and chugged rhythmically from the darkness—darkness lit by a fairytale sprinkle of fireflies.

Places look different at night, but we managed to sneak around the rose garden, past the hedges, and to the Japanese garden and its arched bridge. Overhead, a nearly full moon sailed behind shredded clouds, and trees stood like dark cutouts against the sky. Shifting through the branches, silver light glinted on the coins scattered below us. Taking off our shoes, we stepped into the water.

It wasn't very cold, but the bottom of the pool was slimy. Hoping there wasn't anything too yucky down there, I began picking up coins, slipping them into a pocket. Soon my jeans were soggy but nicely heavy and jingly.

I almost yelled when something brushed past my feet—a huge, ghostly pale goldfish. Moments later, Ethan thrashed a foot and squealed, "Something tried to eat my feet!"

"Relax," I said smugly. "It's just goldfish."

Finally, instead of the excitement of the hunt, I began noticing how heavy and cold my legs felt and how my eyes ached from staring through the moonlight.

"I think that's enough," I said.

"Almost. Looks like a quarter over here."

Climbing out, I sat heavily on a mossy bank. When Ethan joined me, he said, "Should we count our take now?"

"No. A gardener might come by."

"A gardener? At night?"

"Well, maybe a security guard," I answered. "Anyway, if someone catches us, they'd probably

tell our parents."

"Right. We'll count later."

We'd just pulled our socks and shoes onto our wet feet when we heard footsteps on the gravel path. My heart jumped, and I rolled under a sticker bush. Ethan disappeared under a bush beside mine.

The footsteps stopped not far away. I wanted to close my eyes and pretend I wasn't there. Not useful. Instead, I peered between leaves to see if we had any chance of running.

Two dark, portly figures stood on the other side of a low hedge. Moonlight glinted off their bald heads. They weren't looking our way, instead pointing to something high up on the hotel building. I caught a few stray words in their whispered talk: "At the end" and "eliminate" were among them. So were "won't be traced." I thought I heard something about "baiting a trap," but I wasn't sure.

With more gravel crunching, they moved farther along the path and out of sight.

When we finally crawled from our hiding

places, Ethan looked pale, even for him. "They were bald—fat and bald," he whispered.

"So are lots of people," I said, wanting desperately to stay with the pirate-treasure game instead of the alien game. But everything seemed a little less gamelike now.

We stood up and, like deer and things on nature programs, peered around to see if danger had passed. I looked up at the building to see where the men had been pointing. I stifled my gasp, but Ethan had seen it too.

That's where our rooms were. On the top floor at the end.

We didn't speak until we were back in the stairwell, climbing to our floor. "They've found me," Ethan said bleakly.

"They're probably just guys working on fixing up the building," I said firmly.

"At this time of night?"

"So maybe one of them got an idea about something and wanted to show the other? Who knows? Just forget them."

Once back in my room with wet jeans peeled

off and hidden, I couldn't take my own advice. Those fat, bald guys *were* starting to seem sinister. This was stupid—I was letting Ethan's games get to me again.

If they were games.

No! Of course they were! It wasn't aliens he needed protection from. Somehow I had to protect Ethan from his own imagination, just like I'd tried to protect him from bullies.

I groaned and rolled over. There I was again, trying to protect things! Stray cats, lost baby birds—I'd even spent hours picking worms off rain-washed sidewalks and putting them back in the grass. Adults thought that made me a "good citizen." I thought it made me a chump. But I did it anyway; I couldn't help it.

Somewhere in all this thinking, I fell asleep. By morning, everything, even weird guys in dark gardens, seemed less sinister. I pushed their disturbing bits of conversation aside.

Over breakfast, everyone had different ideas about what to do that day. My dad wanted to go to Sunken River Caverns. We had found brochures about it stuck under our doors that morning. Uncle Paul opted for golf, while Mom and Aunt Marsha were all for visiting antique shops. I wanted horseback riding, but Ethan was set on swimming.

After much wild gesturing with buttery toast, we compromised. It was supposed to be sunny today, but rainy tomorrow. So today we'd do outdoors stuff, then visit underground caverns the next day. As for Ethan and me, we'd swim in the morning and in the afternoon head to the stables.

The swimming was okay and so was our pizza lunch, but the afternoon went from bad to worse. A great deal worse. As we headed along the wooded path to the stables, we didn't see a single fat, bald guy, but Ethan walked like it was to his execution.

"Come off it," I said at last. "You're acting as if horses are saber-toothed tigers. A real alien prince would have to get along with different species. Some alien species are a lot odder than horses, I bet."

"Sure, but I wouldn't have to climb on top of them. It's beneath my dignity."

"Dignity, ha! You're just scared."

His pale face flushed red, and I wished I hadn't said that. "Scared has nothing to do with it. I just know the limits of my species. We do not ride other creatures. Period."

I dropped the subject. If he were an alien, I decided, his would be the most pig-headed species in the universe.

When that wonderfully exciting horsey smell greeted us, I left Ethan to gripe about the stink and sit on a bench studying his star guide. Leaning over the fence, I watched the horses and bubbled with envy as a family mounted up for a trail ride.

I'd learned to ride one summer at camp and longed for more chances. So why not now? I slammed a defiant fist against the fence. Ethan could sit around moping over his supposed star home, but I could go riding.

My happy surge of independence fizzled. I couldn't just go off and leave him any more than I could not put out food for stray cats. True, Ethan's parents probably wouldn't care. They seemed to love him, in a vague kind of way, but they usually acted like having a kid was a bother. My parents, though, would chew me out. And even if they didn't, I'd chew myself out.

Efforts to interest Ethan in trying a short, calm-looking palomino failed, so we headed back to the hotel. I stomped along grumpily, imagining myself on the big black stallion I'd seen.

Ethan's thoughts were in their usual orbit. "I still think this pendant has got to be more than just a star map. It must be some sort of weapon. My people would have given me something to protect myself with. Maybe that flying cat was a guardian from my home planet, but maybe he got killed before he could teach me how to use the pendant."

I just grunted. He went on.

"Maybe if I made a big model of all the bumps on the pendant, I'd see a pattern easier. If we do it outside, I could try punching different combinations of bumps on the real pendant and not risk blowing up the hotel if I get it to work."

I didn't even grunt.

We were passing through the woods beside the golf course. Suddenly, Ethan jogged off into a pine grove and started brushing away pine needles with his feet. Reluctantly I helped. I figured I was building ammunition to make him go horseback riding later.

The pine needles gave off a sweet, spicy smell, and dust caught in the shafts of sunlight like flecks of gold. Ethan's pendant glinted fiercely as he set it in the center of the clearing and began arranging rocks and pine cones on the ground, copying its pattern.

I kind of let the angry springs inside me loosen. Sitting back against a pine, I listened to the afternoon woods—a mourning dove calling, insects buzzing, the distant voices of golfers. The air felt warm and drowsy.

With a sudden thump, a white golf ball

bounced into our clearing, knocking aside one of Ethan's pine cones.

He stomped over to replace it, then spun around at the sound of crashing.

Two men stepped out of the bushes. Fat, bald men.

CHAPTER SEVEN

Agent Sorn crouched behind a flowering bush, talking hurriedly into her sender.

"I tapped into meetings and communications, going to great lengths to get our Agent and his family to a new location. To no avail. The Gnairt are here and seem to have identified him."

"Under no circumstances are the Gnairt to capture or injure the boy," Zythis's gargly voice ordered. "His mission is too important to that planet and the Galactic Union."

"Understood. I will attempt to keep him in sight at all times, but these young ones have more energy than Arcturian jiggle bugs. They're hard to keep track of."

"Do whatever is necessary, Agent Sorn."

The connection ended. Still crouching behind the bush, she returned the sender to her satchel, then reluctantly pulled out her silvery laser gun.

"Looking for something, ma'am?"

"Yeek!" The gun arched out of her startled hands, landing deeper in the bushes. She looked up at the gardener, her mind racing though its language implants. "I'm just looking for my ... my ... my hair dryer."

"Whatever. Just don't you hurt the rhododendrons."

"I wouldn't dream of hurting anything, sir."

CHAPTER EIGHT

Maybe I'd been playing too much of this alien stuff, but suddenly our sunny little woods felt a lot colder.

One of the bald men pointed at the golf ball and gave a burbly little laugh. "Sorry to disturb your game, kids, but our game isn't going well either."

I guess that was a joke. The other man laughed. I just stared at the two. They were more than just fat. Their pink skin seemed stretched too tightly over its contents, like over-blown-up balloons. And they were *totally* bald. No eyebrows, no eyelashes, not even a little fringe of hair at the base of their shiny skulls. And even weirder, they were completely identical. Really creepy-looking twins. For a sickening moment, I remembered that the fat, bald guys at the mall had looked like twins too.

So what? The world's full of twins.

Ethan stared at them for a moment too, then hurriedly scooped up his pendant.

"You know, kids," one said in a booming, trying-to-be-jolly voice, "we should join forces. We've lost lots of balls in these woods. If you two pick up all you can find, we'll pay 25 cents a ball. What do you say, kids? You can bring them by our hotel room tonight."

Easy money, all right. There were probably dozens of lost balls in these woods. But, aliens or not, I didn't like these guys. A glance at Ethan's deathly white face cinched it.

"Sorry," I said. "We've got to go."

"Oh, but it's such a lovely afternoon," one balloon-faced man argued, making a practice swing with his golf club. "Tomorrow it may rain."

"In fact, Clyde," the other said, rubbing a bloated hand over his glistening scalp, "let's walk around with them. The woods are cooler than the fairway. They can go after all the balls that old guys like us can't reach."

"Great idea, Bill. What do you say, kids?"

"No," was all Ethan said. I agreed. These guys could be child molesters or something. And the Clyde guy gripped his golf club like he was wielding a weapon.

As we both backed away, I said, "Sorry, no. We've got to get back. Been gone too long already."

We turned and ran down the road, only slowing as we passed someone striding briskly up the path, the white-haired lady from the Vulcan Wasser Pavilion. At the sight of that perfectly normal, smiling person, I suddenly felt foolish. There I was, letting Ethan's crazy game get to me—looking for bad guys everywhere, even in a couple of fat, too-friendly golfers.

During dinner, we could see Clyde and Bill eating at the far end of the dining room, two tables away from the white-haired lady and half hidden by the family we'd seen at the stables. I wondered if we should tell our parents about the two golfers. But tell them what? They hadn't done or even said anything creepy. Well, not very creepy. I sighed. It'd be good when this vacation ended and Ethan wasn't around all the time making me weird.

After dinner, the adults sat on the veranda, and we headed to a spot under the hotel's west tower. The sun had smeared crimson behind a dark wooded ridge. That's where the star guide said Orion could be seen in this time of year.

Ethan babbled on about what his home planet was probably like: his pet flying cats, his mountain palace, his personal rocket scooter. I swung on a bar of the scaffolding that covered that end of the building, and thought about horses.

"Look, you can see stars now," Ethan said excitedly. "I wonder if that's Orion. The pattern looks sort of right."

Glancing at the faint stars near the horizon,

I couldn't see any pattern at all.

"There, just above that pointy tree. That could be home!"

I looked, but it was just a star. Why get excited about a cold distant star when he had an OK home right here? True, I'd rather have my parents than his. But Uncle Paul and Aunt Marsha weren't mean or anything. They were just busy and probably knew more about making money than making kids happy. Besides, who knew what life might be like on that tiny, faraway light? It could be a whole lot worse.

Ethan babbled on. "Sure, that's got to be . . . "

A grating noise came from above. Then a loud crack. I looked up, then dove for Ethan, throwing myself on top of him and a prickly bush. The air sizzled and filled with blue-white light. Then came a crashing thud. For a moment, I was too stunned to move. Ethan squirmed under me. Untangling ourselves, we peered through the fading twilight.

A large building stone had buried itself in

the ground a few feet away.

Fearfully, I looked up. Scaffolding was silhouetted against the violet sky. I thought I saw something else, a head maybe, but then it was gone. "Guess this building does need fixing," I said in a quavery voice. "It's got some major loose stones."

"Loose stones? You've got loose marbles! Someone's trying to kill me."

I didn't feel like arguing. I didn't feel like anything but being safe with our parents on the veranda. At a nervous trot, we headed back but agreed not to tell them about the stone. Otherwise they wouldn't let us out of their sight again. Yet even with them, I didn't quite feel safe. Someone with a rifle could pick us off easily.

This was so dumb! My cousin's not an alien. And nobody's trying to kill him! The fat, bald guys are just creepy humans, and the stone fell by accident. I didn't understand the bit with the light, though. Ethan hadn't seen it because I'd been on top of him. Maybe I'd been hit by a small chunk of rock and "saw stars." Yeah, that was probably it. An accident and a blow to the head.

Once in bed, I kept telling myself the same things over and over. Creepy but human twin golfers. An accident with a building stone. A slight bump on the head—even though I didn't actually feel one. But just the same, I didn't sleep very soon or very well.

CHAPTER NINE

Covered with mud, leaf mold, and stone dust, Agent Sorn paced angrily under the concealing branches of a weeping willow. She jabbed in the sender code of Chief Agent Zythis's message machine, not wanting to explain in real time what had happened.

"Agent Sorn, reporting. The Gnairt have gone too far, attempting to drop a large stone on our Agent. I managed to deflect it with my laser, causing a minor flash. But still, it was a close call. The obvious answer would be to eliminate the Gnairt, but the laws and customs on this planet would call unwanted attention to the killing of two supposed humans, compromising our mission. My only course is to stay close to our Agent and be prepared to act as needed. Out."

She tried to brush the muck off her new, brightly colored native outfit, then gave up. She'd just have to traipse back to the veranda and settle into a rocking chair like a normal, if slightly untidy, resort guest.

This mission was proving to be a lot more trouble than expected. But she admired the young Agent's pluck, even if he had no idea who he really was. She just hoped she could keep him alive.

CHAPTER TEN

The next morning I woke to the sound of rain against the window. No hope for horseback riding today even if I could talk Ethan into it. My dad was pleased, though. Ever since the brochure had appeared under our door, he'd been keen on that underground river trip. He loved that sort of thing and spent most of the short drive to the cave jabbering about blind fish, white crayfish, and other "rare cave fauna."

The place didn't look very promising, just a parking lot and a low cinderblock building. We parked and, when the rain let up a little, made a dash for the building. The next tour wouldn't leave for a half an hour, so we hung out in the gift shop, looking at bat T-shirts, bat refrigerator magnets, and glow-in-the-dark plastic bats.

More people started showing up for the tour. I recognized other resort guests. First was the white-haired pavilion lady. She smiled at us, then began browsing through nature books. After a while came the family with the loud little kids and a dozen or more other folks I didn't recognize. Then, just before time for the tour, the door opened and in stepped the two fat, bald twins, Clyde and Bill. My stomach tightened, and Ethan looked like he was going to throw up.

"They're after me," he whispered.

"No, they're not," I whispered back, hoping I was right. "They're just fat golfers who can't play today because it's raining. Let's just stay away from them."

"The next tour of the magnificent Sunken River Caverns is about to begin," announced a young man in a brown uniform. "Step through the door on your left and guides will take you to the boats."

All the guides were pretty young, like they were high school kids with summer jobs. The rain quit as they trooped us down a steep path. Ahead, the cliff looked like it had had a big bite taken out of it. Ferns and vines grew from its curved, rocky sides. Ethan and I stayed well away from the pudgy twins.

"This part of the state is full of limestone quarries," a guide said, "and honeycombed with caves and underground rivers. But this particular cave wasn't discovered until 1953. That's when a farmer noticed one day that his cow pond had vanished. The weight of the water had collapsed the top of an underground cavern, and the pond and a couple of cows fell into it."

"Did the cows die?" a worried little girl asked.

"Yes," the guide said in a scary voice. "And their ghosts still haunt the cave."

The kid looked like she was going to cry, and the guide quickly said, "Just kidding. Actually the farmer got them out, but he discovered that under his farm was a whole underground river. He and his sons started exploring it, and since then we've mapped miles of underground passages."

"Could more of the cave roof fall in now?" someone asked. I couldn't see through the crowd, but from the oily-sounding voice, it might have been one of the twins. I glanced nervously at Ethan, but he didn't seem to have noticed.

The guide laughed. "If I thought so, I'd find another job. But to be safe, the state bought all the land above the stream system and keeps away heavy activity. Now, walk carefully once you're in the cave. The path's slick with dripping water."

The rain might have stopped, but it was still hot and steamy. Stepping into the cave, though, felt like stepping into an earthy-smelling refrigerator. I was glad I'd believed the brochure and brought a jacket. "Caves keep a constant temperature year round," said the guide. "Early settlers used to store food in them."

As we continued down the steep path, the guide talked about how underground rivers are formed. I was too busy looking to listen much. The rough stone walls glowed with widely spaced electric lights. Occasionally, other passages led off into darkness.

Ethan stuck close to me and as far from Clyde and Bill as possible. When we reached the dock, he whispered, "Let's try for a boat of our own."

A half dozen boats were tied to the wooden dock. Nearest us, a girl guide stepped in and immediately two teenage boys chose that boat too. All the other boats were filling up, so we climbed into hers as well and were soon joined by an Asian couple. At least we weren't sharing a boat with our parents or the fat, bald guys.

One by one, the boats were untied from the dock. Our guide sat in the back, steering and working a quiet electric motor. She talked in a bored voice about blind fish and crayfish, saying that when animals stay out of the sun for generations, they become white and blind. I suppose guides get bored always saying the same stuff, but it actually sounded interesting. I'd have to admit to my dad that this was pretty cool, though not as cool as horseback riding, of course. I watched the black water as the headlight, mounted low on our boat, sliced into it.

Ethan was paying more attention to the other boats. "Our parents are two boats behind us," he whispered. "And the two aliens are way in the back."

I grunted but kept my eyes on the water sliding under us, trying to keep focused on what was the real world. After all, why make up guys from outer space when you're already in a really alien-looking world?

"Hey, there's a blind fish!" I said, pointing at what looked like a bleached goldfish. The guide shone a flashlight on it, but it wasn't bothered by the light. Blind.

The passage the river took narrowed as the guide shone her light over the cave walls, pointing out rock formations with names like "The Camel" or "The Old Man." They kind of looked like those things, but mostly they looked like rocks—rocks that were all melted and twisted like candle wax.

We glided on, seeing more blind fish and several white crayfish looking like tiny ghost lobsters. In the boat behind us, a little girl squealed as something zipped through the air overhead.

"Bats," her guide said. The other kids in that boat started making vampire jokes in really bad Transylvanian accents. Finally someone shushed them.

"This far underground, one of the things you notice, or ought to," our guide said sternly, "is the quiet."

The other guides were saying the same to their boats. The low babble sank to stillness. Total quiet. It was creepy. Then someone banged loudly against the side of a boat. The sound, like cannon fire, rumbled on and on.

"Cave thunder," said our guide. "The rock and water carry sound for miles."

We continued down the cold twisting passage, while our guide chatted with the teenage boys about stuff having nothing to do with caves. Then she raised her voice again.

"As we go by here, you'll feel a slight breeze. We're passing one of the many underground streams that feed into this river. The breeze comes from outside, where a normal surface stream suddenly disappears underground. And now we're coming to the Imperial Cavern."

Ahead of us, the tunnel opened into an underground lake. As the boats glided into it, the guides pointed their big flashlights around. The cave ceiling was high, and rock hung from it in frozen curtains. Water drops glistened at their tips while stumps of rock jutted out of the dark water. Sometimes the two merged into solid pillars. In the center of the lake rose a rock mountain topped with a lump that looked like a throne for some Emperor of the Underworld.

The boats didn't have to keep in line any-more, and they spread out over the dark sur-face of the lake. Our parents waved from their boat, and we waved back. We tried to ignore the boat that held Clyde and Bill. They were the only ones in that boat except for the guide. Guess they reached the weight limit all on their own.

"It was a cavern like this," the chief guide announced, "that used to be under the farm pond. Today, you could walk through the woods above us and never know that this fan-tastic underground world was here. Now we're going to show you something you seldom get to see on the surface. This is what pure dark is like."

Suddenly, all the lights on the boats switched off. This was dark. Majorly dark. I waved my hands in front of my face but couldn't see a flicker.

Nervous whispers echoed around the cavern. Then a mournful call silenced the rest. Low and sad, it recalled every ghost story I'd ever heard.

"The ghosts of the lost cows!" a deep voice intoned. That set off one kid's scream and a bunch of giggles. Soon the cavern echoed with less-than-ghostly mooing.

"So, that's a cave fish's view of the world," a guide said as the lights came back on.

A moment earlier, I had been staring at blackness. Suddenly, I found myself looking right at the boat carrying Clyde and Bill. I saw more than their gross shapes and shiny heads. I saw what one held in his hand. Something metallic. Something that looked like a gun.

What happened next took seconds. But I remember it in very slow motion.

CHAPTER ELEVEN

When the lights switched back on, I was the only one looking toward the fat, bald guys. The glinting gun pointed in our direction. Grabbing Ethan, I threw us both to the bottom of the boat. At the same time, a twin raised the gun higher. He wasn't aiming at us but at the cave ceiling.

Was it just a camera? No. I heard a crack—sort of like gunfire. But what came from the barrel was no bullet. It wasn't flame or light either, but more like a stream of air above a candle—air quivering with heat.

It sliced into the rock above us. An explosive

rumble filled the cavern. People screamed. The rock groaned. Flashlight beams darted upward, catching a huge slab of rock shuddering loose. More screams. The guide and the two teens leaped off one side of our boat and the Asian couple off the other.

"Mom! Dad!" Ethan called, lurching to his feet. The boat rocked. I tackled him around the waist and leaped off the back. Cold black water closed over us. A sound like thunder crashed. The empty boat bobbing behind us splintered under cascading rock. A huge wave lifted us like driftwood, washing us back toward the tunnel.

The cavern filled with noise. People screamed as more rock broke loose. A few beams of light zigzagged about. The two of us smashed onto a slick, flat rock that was just under the water. Crouching on it like a toad, Ethan started to yell. I slapped my hand over his mouth.

By the frantic beams of light darting through the darkness, I could see one boat moving closer. Not a rescue boat. Clyde and Bill were

steering it. Their guide was gone.

"They want to finish us," I whispered. Tugging on Ethan's arm, I slid silently into the water. He didn't need more urging. Keeping our heads just above water, we paddled back into the mouth of the tunnel.

From the wet darkness, I looked back. Clyde and Bill, in their boat, were examining the wreck of ours. A metallic something still glinted in one of their hands. Then their flashlight began skimming over the water in our direction. We slipped behind a big rock and kept swimming.

In the chaos behind us, I could hear our parents calling our names. We didn't dare answer. I couldn't hear its electric motor but was sure Clyde and Bill's boat was heading our way. The passage ahead was dark. It still echoed with the thunderous explosion. Pulling myself half onto a rock, I tried to remember the way this tunnel had looked just before we'd entered the cavern. Was there any place to hide?

I shivered as a cold draft played over my skin.

"The side passage!" I whispered, slipping again into the dark water. With Ethan close behind me, we floundered into even deeper darkness. A faint current in the water showed I was right. A side stream entered somewhere nearby.

Ahead, a break in the rock wall was low and tumbled with boulders. We'd just pulled ourselves behind them as a lit boat glided silently by in the main passage.

This was an underground creek, not a river, shallow enough to walk in—or rather duck-walk since the ceiling was too low for standing.

"What do we do now?" Ethan whispered, his scared voice barely rising above the noise from the cavern.

"We can't go back in there yet. Those two are looking for us." I thought a moment. "In fact, when they don't find our bodies or catch up to us in the main passage, they may remember this side stream. Let's follow it. Quickly.

The guide said it leads outside."

That sounded simple enough. It wasn't. As we moved farther back, the last trace of light from the cavern vanished. It was as dark as it had been during that tour demonstration. The dry rock beside us was as raspy as sandpaper. The rocks below were slippery with cold, wet slime.

After a while, the scared energy that had been driving me faded. I was almost numb from cold, and my arms and legs were shaking and bruised from banging into rocks.

"Let's rest a minute," I gasped when I found myself on a dry, flattish rock. "I can't see or hear anything coming after us."

I felt Ethan crawl up beside me. He was shivering. I put an arm around him.

"I'm sorry, little cousin," I forced myself to say. I felt almost as numb from the truth as from the cold. "I never really believed you like I should have. Those guys *were* trying to kill you, and they have weapons like people... like *humans* just don't have."

"They *are* aliens, aren't they?" he said faintly.

I nodded, but of course he couldn't see that. I said what I didn't want to hear. "And I guess you are too. I wish I'd believed you earlier. You probably *are* some sort of lost alien prince."

"I don't . . . I wasn't . . . " He choked to a stop, his body shaking now like he was crying. Suddenly, he pushed himself off the rock.

"Let's go. We can't let them catch us!"

His clattering and splashing showed he was moving faster than he should in this dark. "Slow down!" I hissed. "Make that much noise, and they'll hear us."

He seemed to slow but was still ahead of me. Passing him up, I bumped my head. The ceiling was getting lower. The farther we went, the lower it got, forcing us to crawl. I started

feeling like the whole mountainside was pressing down on me. If it hadn't been for the cool breeze I might have panicked and fled back to face the aliens. But then, I had another alien here to try and protect.

As we floundered on, I heard new rumbling. Was more of the cavern caving in? Were our parents and all those other people all right?

Suddenly, my attention snapped back to us. Either the water was getting higher or the ceiling was getting a lot lower. There wasn't much room between the two any more. Like salamanders, we half swam, half crawled along the stream. The current was strong, but when we tried to lift ourselves out of it, we scraped against rough rock. And now that rock ceiling was wet. At times there might be nothing but water in this little tunnel. We could drown!

The rumbling was louder. It sounded like... like thunder. Maybe it was raining again outside. That's why the stream was rising!

"Hurry!" I said as water sloshed into my

mouth. I jerked and scraped my head on rock.

Ethan got the point. I could hear him scooting behind me. In fact, when I looked back, I could almost see him. A black shape against lesser black. Were we coming to daylight?

My battered head pressed against the ceiling, and water nearly blinded me. But there was light ahead. I grabbed a breath between waves and scrambled on. Suddenly, water was coming from above as well. Out of a thunderous gray sky, rain poured down on us. I'd never felt anything so welcome in my life!

"Over here!" Ethan had rushed out. His voice now came from my left. "There's a kind of shelter."

Staggering to stand up, I stumbled his way. Soon we were crouched side by side under a rock ledge. It wasn't much protection. A strong wind battered the rain right onto us.

Like a frog, Ethan scrambled further left. "It's better over here. Almost dry."

At the back of the overhang, the ground

was dusty and scattered with dry leaves. I wondered briefly about wild animals but decided they'd be better than torrential rain or murderous aliens.

For a while, we huddled in silence. Ethan was shivering again, and there was enough light to see he was crying. I put an arm around him.

"Next time you tell me anything, Ethan, I promise I'll believe you. Unicorns in your backyard—anything."

"But you shouldn't!" he sobbed. "You shouldn't have believed me. I didn't, not deep down. I knew it was sort of a game, but I wanted it to be true. So I pretended harder and harder until I almost believed it. But now... now I don't want it to be true. I don't want to be an alien! I want to be just an ordinary kid with ordinary parents. I know they're not great parents, but they're *human*. I want to be human too!"

He curled up in a ball and shook with sobs. I held him tight, crying a little too. Sure, boys aren't supposed to cry, but they aren't supposed to go through stuff like this either. I was worried about my parents. I was worried those ghastly bloated aliens would track us down. And most of all, I was worried about my crazy alien cousin. He was the real thing.

The rain looked like it would never let up. No one could move in a torrent like that, so I guessed we were safe enough for the moment. After a while, exhausted and huddled together in our cold dry den, we both fell asleep.

It may have been hours later when we woke up. The sky beyond the rocky ledge was clotted with dark clouds that flashed and rumbled. But the rain had stopped.

I started to move, then froze. Against the lightening-lit sky, I saw something. A dark, standing shape.

CHAPTER TWELVE

The dark figure snorted and swayed as it stood against the sky. Not an alien . . . a bear! Big improvement. I should have known sheltering in a cave was a bad idea.

Beside me, Ethan whimpered and pulled his knees up to his chin. The creature dropped to all fours and began waddling away. I blinked, trying to get the scale of the thing. Too small for a bear. It looked back at us, black eyes glinting from a mask of dark fur. Dark fur striped the bushy tail. A raccoon!

Ethan began giggling. And soon we were both gasping with laughter, loud enough to drive away a herd of bears. Or attract a couple of aliens.

"Quiet!" I whispered sharply. "They may still be looking for us."

That shut down the laughing. "They may use some alien device to track us down," Ethan whispered. "We've got to go!"

Ethan stood up quickly, grazing his head on the rocky roof. I stood cautiously. "Yeah, but we can't just run. We've got to think first. Other people could be looking for us too—our parents and the police or park rangers."

Ethan walked nervously to the edge of the overhang and looked out. "But they may think we were crushed by that falling rock and be looking for our bodies in there. Clyde and Bill must have seen us jump off, or they wouldn't have followed us up the passage. The guide in their boat probably mentioned that side stream too. They could be following us now!"

"They're too fat for that route," I pointed out. "But maybe they've left the cave and are trying to find where that side passage comes out.   Let's move!   If we can just find other people before those guys find us, we should be all right."

As we stepped from under the ledge, hanging ferns scattered raindrops on us. The dark clouds were moving farther away, but the sky was not very comforting. It was pink with sunset. Soon it would be night.

"How are we going to find anything in the dark?" Ethan whimpered.

I looked down at the stream that bubbled past us before dropping into the little cave we'd crawled from. "Just follow the stream. That'll keep us from walking around in circles like they say happens when you're lost in the woods. The stream's bound to run into a road or bridge sooner or later."

Following the stream wasn't hard at first. There was still enough pinkish light from the sunset sky. But soon it was harder not to trip over roots or get entangled in briars. From the darkening forest around us came sounds of frogs, insects, and mournful birds. The cool air smelled wet and moldy. Sometimes noisy things, raccoons or whatever, crashed through the bushes. We froze for frightened moments, scarcely daring to breathe.

Just as I was beginning to think we'd have to give up and find someplace to hide for the night, a full moon edged into sight beyond the trees. Its silvery pale light shifted with the wind-stirred leaves, showing us where to put our feet.

Soon afterward the little stream spread out into a reedy pool below a cliff and disappeared.

"I don't get it," Ethan complained. "How can a stream just stop?"

I looked at the base of the cliff where bubbles, silvered by the moonlight, rose through the dark water. "Maybe it starts here, from an underground spring. Bummer. Now we've got to follow something else."

What I really wanted to do was cry like a baby and wait till my mother found me. We were lost, in the woods, at night. That was nightmare enough—even without murderous aliens. But I was the big kid here, the one supposed to look out for his little cousin. And, alien or not, he was still family.

I looked around. "Okay, this cliff will do. Follow it until we find a house or something. Then someone will call the police for us, and everything will be all right." I tried to sound as if I believed that.

Following the cliff was not easy. Rocks were tumbled along its base, and if we moved away too far, we lost sight of the cliff behind the trees. But then the ground became more even and open. It was Ethan who figured out why.

"Hey, Zack, I think we're on a road!"

I stopped and looked around. It was hard to be sure of anything among the jumbled shadows and moonlight, but along a strip in two directions there were no trees. The ground was hard with gravel.

"You're right! Doesn't look like it's been used for years, but it's got to lead somewhere!"

We moved on with hopeful steps, occasionally

scrambling over fallen trees. Then the road divided.

The track to the left was more overgrown, so we turned right. We hadn't gone far before we stopped, rooted with fright. Something was crashing through the woods. Something big. It was getting closer. I was too scared to run or hide or do anything except hope that whatever it was didn't see us.

A big buck burst from the trees ahead of us. With only a fleeting glance, it charged past us down the road.

Ethan laughed nervously. "A deer. It sounded like Godzilla."

"Or like Godzilla was after it," I joked. Not a very good joke. What could scare a deer that badly? After all, it lived in the night woods all the time. It wouldn't get spooked by a raccoon. But a real bear? Maybe. Or worse.

"Let's hurry," I said. "I'm getting really hungry.

"Right. I could eat ten triple cheeseburgers and a carload of fries. What do you . . . "

I grabbed his arm to silence him, then pointed. Off to our right, where the deer had come from, a light moved in the forest. A flashlight maybe. Rescuers? There was something wrong about the light, though. It had kind of an odd violet tinge, like lights in science demonstrations that make rocks glow.

"If they're rescuers, they should be calling our names," Ethan whispered.

"And they should be using ordinary flashlights," I added. "Back to the other road!" Hurrying back to where our road forked, we took the overgrown way. We weren't much quieter than that panicky deer.

Our track ran along the bottom of a small canyon. On either side rose piles of squared boulders covered with vines. The road widened, and we began to run, then grabbed at each other, stumbling to a stop. A few feet ahead of us, the road ended. Beyond it and way below it, moonlight glinted on water. Green, deep-looking water.

Inching forward, we peered over the edge.

The pool was large with squared, rocky sides. In fact, all around and above us, rock cliffs and ledges looked oddly even and blocky. Suddenly, I remembered a field trip from last year.

"An old quarry," I whispered. "That's what the road must have been built for."

"So the way *out* of the woods will be the other direction—where the light's coming from."

I looked around. The shadows among the giant stone blocks were inky black. "Let's hide. Maybe whatever it is will go past."

We skirted the edge of the drop-off and took shelter behind a wall of huge tumbled stones. Several leaned together to make a tent of darkness. Ethan dashed toward it, but I whispered, "Wait! There might be snakes."

Grabbing a stick off the ground, I rattled it around in the dark space, though whether this would make snakes leave or get mad, I didn't know. When nothing happened, we stepped inside.

Crouching in the dark, we listened. An owl called not far away, and frogs or insects with big throaty voices creaked and chugged from the water below. The smell of wild roses drifted through the night. Time oozed past. I was about to suggest we go, when the rhythmic chugging from the pond stopped. Ominous silence was broken by a faint crunching of gravel.

I peered out of our shelter. On the pale stone around us, I could see a faint violet glow. Quickly I drew back. Shadows moved eerily over the rock as the light slowly shifted. They must be using some sort of weird flashlight, I realized, one that helped their alien eyesight. Then a voice broke the stillness.

"No need to hide any longer. We know you're there. Come out now and make this easier."

"No way," Ethan muttered behind me. I shook my head, afraid they might have super-alien hearing. Apparently they didn't.

The voice came again, from further away. "You can't hide—we'll find you. And you can't fight because you haven't learned to use the power yet. If you give up now, we'll let you live.   We'll take you away from here—back where you belong."

I tensed up. Ethan just might fall for that. But he didn't. "I don't belong with murdering monsters like them," he muttered. "Let's find a better hiding place."

He slipped away before I could stop him. But he was right. It wouldn't be hard to track us down here.

Ethan had disappeared around another square-cut boulder. I followed to find him scrambling up a crevice in a rocky cliff. Might as well quit worrying about snakes, I decided. At least snakes were from Earth.

Vines and tree roots made it easier to climb than I'd thought. Nature had been busy re-claiming the sides of this quarry. I joined Ethan on a shallow ledge, then pulled us both down flat. A circle of violet light was moving from behind a rock.

Like lizards, we crawled along the ledge to a shadowed corner. Then, wedging ourselves be-tween rock and the trunk of a young pine, we worked our way up to the next ledge.

This ledge was deeper, and at the back a cleft in the rock made a small cave. Crouching there, I wished I'd some clue what this place looked like in daylight. All we were doing was taking the first route we saw to get higher and farther away. But we could be trapping ourselves as easily as escaping.

The silence stretched on. I peered down at the quarry below. In the moonlight, the limestone looked ghostly white, with sharp rock edges outlined in deepest shadow. We could have been in some ruined jungle temple. And I wished we were. I'd take cobras, panthers, and angry tribespeople any time.

"If we can climb to the top of the quarry hole," Ethan whispered, "maybe we can lose them in the woods."

I wasn't sure I wanted to leave this hiding place. If only the enemy would give some sign of where they were. But Ethan was already scuttling along this one ledge and pulling himself up to another one.

Just as I reached that second ledge, the air above us quivered. With a splintering crack, a rock overhead shattered and rained down in sharp, hot chunks.

We huddled together, arms thrown over our heads. Again the voice echoed over the quarry.

"If you make it easier to kill you than capture you, we will! But if you want to live, come down. You might as well. You know you don't belong here. We can take you where you do belong. We can take you home!"

In a shadowed corner of rock, Ethan suddenly stood up. "Forget it, turkeys! I belong here! Maybe this wasn't always my home, but it is now. Go back to wherever you come from and leave me alone!"

I felt proud of him and wished he'd shut up at the same time. But I didn't have much time for either thought.

Violently, the air quivered. The far end of our ledge exploded into stinging gravel. When I could open my eyes against the dust,

I saw Ethan fumbling at the pendant around his neck.

"They said I hadn't learned how to use the power yet. But I've tried. If only I had more time!"

Beyond his crouching figure, I saw that the blast seemed to have opened a new escape route.

"Forget the pendant. Move!" I barked, pushing him ahead of me down a narrow channel in the rock. After a few feet, he squealed and stopped dead.

"Whoa! End of the line!"

I peered around him. There was nothing there. A sheer cliff dropped down to water. Dark, silent water, too dark for even the moonlight to knife into.

For seconds, I felt hopelessly trapped. But neither of us was the giving-up sort. The rocky groove that we'd followed was slightly higher than our heads. Ethan fumbled at its rough sides, trying to find footholds. I knelt down, let him stand on my knee, and gave him a boost up. He flailed and shoved but finally pulled himself out. Then he swiveled around and reached down for me.

After I'd made the top, we crouched low and ran across this new ledge. It ended suddenly. A dozen feet below was another ledge. Between the two stretched a pine tree growing stubbornly in some shallow pocket of soil. For a moment, Ethan looked frantically about. Then, like a panicky squirrel, he leaped across to the tree and started clambering down.

I crouched, ready to follow. Again a wave of quivering air shot toward us. It slammed into the base of the tree. Sawdust and splinters billowed upward. The tree toppled onto the ledge below us.

Ethan's scream was short and terrified. Its echoes died, and the quarry settled into silence. Deathly silence.

CHAPTER THIRTEEN

I don't know how I got down there. I was too scared to think. Somehow, I just scrambled down to that lower ledge. Ethan had rolled away from the ruined pine, almost to the rim of the ledge. He was lying very still.

I crouched over him. He was still breathing, but his pale face was flecked with blood, and his eyes were closed. At least the broken pine branches hid us from below, not that they would do much good against the enemy's pulverizing gun.

"Ethan," I whispered frantically, "wake up! Please. Don't let them catch you. You can still get away!"

Nothing. Not a flicker. He lay there pale, bloodied, and still. Like a little dead bird.

If only I'd believed him, really believed him, earlier. Maybe I could have done more to protect him.

"Come on, Ethan, wake up. I won't let them get you! I love you, Ethan. You're my cousin. It doesn't matter that you're an alien. Your mom and dad love you too. You're family! You belong with us. Please, wake up!"

I ruffled his hair and patted his face, but nothing changed. Anxiously I looked around. Maybe I could carry him. The ledge we were on stretched to the left, then turned a sharp corner. Maybe . . . I froze.

On the far side of the quarry something was moving along the cliff face, something with a faint violet light. One of those fat guys climbing a cliff? Still, under all their seeming flub might be alien muscle.

I flattened myself on the ledge beside Ethan, but soon the figure would be high enough to see us. Could I drag Ethan farther behind the fallen pine? I reached for him and caught sight of the chain around his neck. Quickly I slipped it and the pendant over his head. It glinted like fire in the moonlight. There had to be some way to make this thing work!

I held it away from me, frantically poking the little knobs. The violet light on the opposite cliff was climbing higher. I looked again at Ethan. It might not be safe to move him, but it wouldn't be safe much longer leaving him here. I rose to a crouch and grabbed his shoulders.

Crackling air skimmed over me. Fallen pine branches burst into a rain of needles and sawdust.

"Time's up, kid," the alien's voice boomed. "Guess you'll have to stay here dead."

I spun around, about to yell back something when another voice called sharply, "Guess again!"

A beam of blue-white light shot across the quarry into the climbing figure. Something screamed, something not human. Seconds later a charred, twisted shape fell to the dark waters below.

Stunned, I looked toward the source of the beam. Someone was standing on the rim of the quarry. A slender figure. Rescuers! The police had finally tracked us down. But that weapon . . . what was that?

The new figure was moving our way. Then it left the rim and began climbing down the rock face. Whoever it was, he was a very good climber. Nervously I looked around. There was still one fat alien left.

At one end of the quarry, our rescuer reached a ledge and leaped from it to an angled block of stone. Just then, a shaft of wavering air shot across the quarry and smashed into that block. It heaved sideways, and the person clinging to it was thrown backwards. That last shot, I realized, had come from almost underneath us.

Crawling to the rim of our ledge, I cautiously stuck my head over. The other alien and his violet light were moving below and to my right.

Sitting back, I looked to the far end of the quarry. Our rescuer was still there but seemed to be caught in a rock crevice or something. I could see arms flailing.

And here I was, helplessly watching! Desperate, I grabbed at the pendant again. *It's got to work!* I yelled in my mind. *It's supposed to have some power, so let's see it!*

Clutching the metal disk, I leaned over the rock edge. As if it were a gun, I aimed the disk at the figure silently climbing below me. My mind was yelling orders as I jabbed randomly at the crystal and knobs. *That power, I need that power! I've got to save our rescuer! I've got to save Ethan! I need help!*

I squeezed the pendant so hard my fingers tingled. No, it was the light, the light that made them tingle. My whole hand was glowing with pale blue light!

My fingertips glowed brighter and brighter, throbbing with pain, burning pain. Then, like glowing needles, the light shot beyond them. It shot down the cliff. The climbing alien shrieked. I couldn't see beyond the flare of light, but something splashed into the water far below.

Stunned, I pulled back my hand and stared at it. The glow was gone. So, almost, was the pain. There were no scars, no burns. The pendant hung dully from the chain wrapped around my wrist.

That's when I began shaking. Shaking uncontrollably. I'd used an alien weapon. I'd killed an alien. I'd saved my cousin. I'd saved that other person. I was going to be sick!

Dizzily I rolled over and retched. Again and again, my body convulsed. Nothing much came out, but finally I felt better. Weak and dizzy, but better.

Minutes passed. I was lying on my back staring vaguely at the stars when a figure came between me and them. Someone helped me sit up.

"So, you learned to use the power."

"Yeah," I said weakly. "But it's not my... Ethan! Will he be all right?"

The stranger nodded. "I checked him over. He's scratched and battered, but he'll be fine. He'll wake up soon."

I looked at our rescuer and realized I'd seen her before. Somewhere. Yes. The white-haired lady from the Vulcan Wasser Pavilion, the one who'd also been on the boat trip! Her hair might be white, but clearly she wasn't old or feeble.

"What . . . how . . . who . . . ?" I stuttered, then tried again. "You're an alien too, aren't you?"

She smiled. "Of course. My name is Agent Sorn. And I apologize. We didn't suspect things were going wrong, or we would have stepped in earlier."

I looked at my cousin lying peacefully on the rock. "Are you going to take Ethan away?" I felt heavy waiting for the answer.

"Your cousin? Why should I take him away?"

"Well, I mean, if he's a lost alien prince or something, and the bad guys have found him,

won't you have to hide him somewhere else?
Or is it time to go back to his home planet
anyway?"

For a moment she looked puzzled. Then
she laughed. A sharp birdlike sound, it finally
died into little chuckles. "I see what you
must have been thinking. But no, your cousin's not an alien."

"He's not?"

"No. You are."

CHAPTER FOURTEEN

After everything that had been happening lately, you'd think nothing could surprise me. But those words sure did. They bounced around my mind but wouldn't sink in.

"What was that again?"

"You are the alien here," the woman said calmly. "When your parents adopted you, they didn't realize you weren't human, of course. Not even most doctors could tell. When we do an Agent Project, we choose representatives from compatible species."

More words that weren't sinking in. But something had. One word jabbed like a chip of ice. "I'm adopted?" That one word, and I felt like my brain had just exploded. My world certainly had.

"That's the standard procedure. It's important that the Agent be raised as if he, she, or it belongs on that planet—raised to be totally part of its culture."

I must have looked as stunned and confused as I felt. She stopped and said, "I'm not explaining this very well, am I?"

Numbly I shook my head.

"The problem is that I shouldn't be explaining this at all—not now, anyway. Usually we let Agents fully mature in their adopted cultures before they're told of their true natures. Ideally, we would have waited until you were in your twenties."

I stared at her, still not getting much of this. "Maybe you could start by explaining who this 'we' is."

"The Galactic Union. When a planet's civilization becomes advanced enough, it is invited to join. The problem is, many species become very disturbed when they first learn they aren't the most important thing in the universe— that there are thousands of other intelligent species, some of which are very different from themselves. We've found that the best way to open contact is to have an Agent on the planet who totally understands the local culture, who can act as an intermediary between the Galactic Union and the natives. So when the time is right, we introduce an Agent, as an infant, into a normal native family and let it mature and learn there."

"Oh." I shook my head, trying to get things to settle. Better go at this piece by piece. "So who are . . . were the fat, bald guys?"

She frowned. "Unfortunate. They were Gnairt. Gnairt are a piratical species who like to exploit planets before they are ready to join the Galactic Union. They want to keep Earth out longer so they can steal its natural resources and profit from private trading deals. Once they learned the Union had already planted its Agent here, their aim was to find and remove him."

"Me."

She sighed. "Our fault, really. We had no idea the Gnairt were interested in this planet. It's rather out of their way. If we'd known there were Gnairt operatives here, we wouldn't have left you unprotected for so long."

Beside me on the ledge, Ethan moaned and shifted slightly. I looked down at him. "So, Ethan's idea that he's an alien was just crazy make-believe?"

"Not crazy, really," she chuckled. "Wanting to be something special, something different is common enough among any species. But someone like him could never have been our Agent. We choose our Agents carefully and place them with equal care. Your true genetic species has a strong streak of responsibility and protectiveness. And the adoptive parents we found for you are loving and ideally suited to bring out those traits. We need our Agents to grow up happy with themselves, their families, and their lives. Your cousin isn't like that."

"But why did he choose that particular . . . ?" A memory slammed into me. "Oh. When we were little—the cat. He decided he was an alien *after* we met that cat. It really did talk and have wings?"

The woman nodded. "A feline Agent sent to check on you. Unfortunately it was attacked by some sort of native carnivore and inadvertently gave itself away—to your cousin, anyway."

Pieces were shakily falling into place. But something still wasn't right. "Then what about the pendant?" I held it out to her. "Ethan had it since he was a baby, and just now I used it as some kind of weapon. That's no ordinary piece of junk jewelry."

The woman looked it over and shook her head. "But it is. The pendant's ordinary. It's *you* who aren't. You were the weapon. The power came from you."

The truth jolted through me. "You mean when those alien guys were yelling about not having learned to use the power yet, they were really yelling at *me*? They meant power . . . inside me?"

"Exactly. That's another thing we would have taught you when you were old enough. We didn't think there was any chance of you stumbling upon it accidentally. But kids here on Earth usually don't face this much stress and danger. That's what brought it out. You saved all of our lives with that power. But I warn you, don't even try using it again before you're properly taught. It can be dangerous to you as well as others."

"I can believe that." The dizziness still hadn't left me. For a minute, I just stared out at the quarry and its crazy pattern of light and shadow. The pattern of my own life suddenly seemed as crazy. But at least I was beginning to see it.

I sighed. "So what happens now?"

"You two return to your families and go about your lives. Forget about being an Agent for a while, just enjoy your life as a human. We'll start your training earlier than planned, perhaps, but until then you deserve to lead a normal life. Don't worry, though, we'll keep much closer watch on things here."

The woman stood up. "On the immediate front, let's get you back to civilization. Your families are going crazy with worry, and several search teams are out."

With that, she reached down and scooped Ethan up as if he weighed nothing at all. Then throwing him over her shoulder, she started scrambling up the rock face. I just stood staring.

Halfway up, she turned and called. "Come on, you can do it. Don't think about it, just climb."

That must have been how I got down to this ledge in the first place. If I'd thought about it, I'd have been too scared.

All right, I said to myself. *Alien powers, if you're there, get on with it!*

Trying not to think, I just climbed the rock. Somehow finding hand and footholds, I moved steadily upward until we were at the top.

Tangled, shadowy woods sloped away from us. Crickets chirped and an owl called from a distant tree. The breeze hinted of pine and honeysuckle. Forcing our way through bushes and over fallen logs, we finally reached the old road.

Gently, the woman laid Ethan down in a nest of gnarled roots. She placed her hands above Ethan's body and moved them from his head to his feet. I thought I caught a bit of glow coming from her hands. "He'll wake soon and be fine. I don't suppose I have to caution you not to tell him or anyone else what I've told you?"

"No. I understand." As if anyone would believe me. Well, Ethan might. But it could hurt him too—giving up his specialness to someone else.

I looked at the woman as a foggy idea formed in my head. "Here, could you take this with you? I don't want to lie about everything." I handed her Ethan's pendant.

She nodded and took a ring off her finger. "An exchange then. Just a bauble I picked up

at a space-station gift shop. Powerless, but pretty—and authentic alien."

I took the rainbow shifting ring, admiring the colors.

"I've got to go now, Zack," the woman said. "They'll find you soon. But don't worry, we'll be in touch."

She started down the overgrown road, then she turned. "You know, I envy you. This is a good planet to belong to. A good place to call home."

Almost before her footsteps had died away, Ethan was stirring at my feet. I crouched beside him, my thoughts tossing about like a sick person. He opened his eyes. I took a deep breath.

"Hey, Ethan, glad you're back."

He sat up and looked blearily around. "What happened? I was climbing down a tree, and one of those baddies shot at it. But that wasn't here."

"No, another alien carried you out. She explained everything. You were right about lots of stuff. I should have believed you. There are good aliens and bad aliens." I paused a minute, rummaging through ideas. Then I stumbled ahead.

"But they weren't after you, really, they were after . . . your pendant. It's really powerful. It seems that years ago some aliens crash landed on Earth. They had this important pendant with them, and before some bad guys could track them down, they hid it with a toddler they met in a park. They begged you to protect it. Maybe it was ESP or something, but you did."

Ethan's eyes were wide. My mind kept leaping ahead, interweaving fact and fantasy. "But the bad aliens figured out what had happened to it. That's why they were after you. After they knocked that tree down, one of the good aliens arrived, a lady with terrific white hair, and blasted them with this really cool ray thing. Then she carried you out here. She said you'd be fine."

"And the pendant?" he said fumbling at his

neck. "Is it safe?"

"Yes. She took it. It can go back to its home planet now. But she thanked you for being its guardian all these years. She said how proud they all were of you. And she wanted you to have this."

I handed him the ring. In the moonlight, color shifted over it like oil on water. He slipped it on a finger.

"Wow," I laughed. "You'll be the only kid on your block to have a real alien ring!"

He smiled, then looked at me, smiling even broader. "So I'm not an alien! I was taking care of an alien pendant, but I'm really *human*. I belong here!"

His words tore at me, but I nodded. "Yes, Ethan, and I'm glad. I don't want my favorite cousin snatched away to some weird alien planet. Your parents would feel the same, too."

"My parents! So they really *are* my parents." His voice trembled a bit. "You know, Zack, I've got to admit, I'm kind of glad. They're not perfect, but they're family." He wrapped me in a quick hug.

"So, let's see if we can find them." I stood up, feeling painfully hollow. Ethan had found his family, but had I lost mine? I thought about my home, about my parents—my adoptive parents, but the only ones I had ever known.

No, I insisted fiercely. We had all loved my crazy cousin even when he thought he was an alien. And I loved him still. I loved them all. That made them family enough.

I turned back to where he sat, looking pale and happy in the moonlight. I smiled. "The alien lady said teams are out looking for us. If we head down the road, maybe we'll meet them. But we'd better keep this alien stuff secret. Who would believe it, anyway?"

It would take me a while to believe it myself.

The sky beyond the trees was beginning to gray with dawn, but in the woods it was still dark enough for flashlights. It wasn't long before we saw some weaving toward us. Beams of yellow-white light. Regular Earth flashlights.

"Mom, Dad, we're here!" Ethan yelled, running on ahead.

I followed more slowly. A new world was still arranging itself in my head. This was like a page in a puzzle book, I thought suddenly. *Which cousin is the real alien?*

Laughing, I hurried forward. Neither is, really. We both belong here. True, one of us has a little different background and a different job ahead. But right now, I wanted my family. I wanted to go home.

The adventure
continues...

camp aLien

[BOOK #2 OF THE
aLien agent
series]

pamela F. service
illustrated by mike gorman

TOP SECRET from CAMP ALIEN

"But this is crazy!" I told Sorn. "Kids on Earth can't just take off on secret missions without adults asking questions and probably saying no."

"We've taken care of that," she answered. "You'll be leaving shortly for a site near where we believe the Duthwi eggs were dumped, somewhere just east of Lake Takhamasak. Our Cadet will meet you there with further details."

Suddenly I felt like I'd been dumped out of the Ferris wheel. "Wait a minute! You had me turned down by Camp Trailblazer and sent to Camp Takhamasak instead!"

"Rather clever, I thought, for such short notice."

"But it's not fair! I didn't choose to . . ."

She fixed me again with those amethyst eyes. "Zack, few of us of whatever species have complete free choice over our lives. You can choose not to help, if you want, but I imagine that after living on this planet all your life, you might care enough about it to choose saving it from harm."

I swallowed like I was fighting motion sickness. She had me there. Maybe I was an alien, but I didn't feel like one. Earth was my home, and if I could keep some nasty aliens from messing it up, I guess I had to try.